HUGH PINE

Now there's one very important characteristic all porcupines have, and that's stubbornness. If there's something a porcupine really wants, he'll get it, even if it's a piece of rye bread you've left on your kitchen table. He'll get in through the window and grab it and waddle right out the door, while you stand there hopping up and down screaming at him. You can break the broom on his back and he'll still waddle on, waving his tail at you, and his tail is nothing to be sneezed at. It's thick and strong and full of sharp quills that will stick in the broom handle so that you'll need a pair of pliers to get them out.

HUGH PINE

by Janwillem van de Wetering

Illustrated by Lynn Munsinger

Beech Tree Books • New York

Library of Congress Cataloging in Publication Data

Van de Wetering, Janwillem, 1931-
Hugh Pine.

SUMMARY: Hugh Pine, a porcupine genius, works
with his human friends to save his less intelligent
fellow porcupines from the deadly dangers of the road.
[1. Porcupines – Fiction. 2. Safety – Fiction]
I. Munsinger, Lynn. II. Title.
PZ7.V2852Hu [Fic] 80-13652

First Beech Tree Edition, 1992.

ISBN 0-688-11799-6

2 4 6 8 10 9 7 5 3 1

HUGH PINE

Chapter One

MAYBE, IF YOU have nothing to do one day, you could go north, and if you do, and keep a little east as well, you will, just before you get out of the country altogether, reach a town called Rotworth. It isn't much of a town, and if you were going fast you might not even see it. But it's there, with its two stores, and its church, and the post office that belongs to old Mr. McTosh, and the Peacock Dairy, and a few other buildings that have long since lost their signs. And just after you have gone through Rotworth, if you take a left and travel on, a few miles only, you will get to Sorry.

Nobody lives in Sorry; nobody but Hugh Pine, that is. When you ride the Sorry road you may see him walking along under his big red floppy hat, which hangs down and covers most of his face and leaves the rest in a shadow. You can see his white whiskers sticking out from under the hat, so you know he is old, and you can see his thick coat, so you may suppose that he feels cold, as many old people do even on a hot day. You'll wave at him, of course; everybody waves at each other up there in the Northeast, for there aren't that many people about, and it's nice to know that you aren't alone.

Hugh Pine always waves back. The people from Rotworth used to think (they know better now), "Hey, that must be that little old man who lives up in Sorry in the woods somewhere and grows or catches his own food, for he never comes to the two stores of Rotworth." And then they'd forget him again, and that's just what Hugh Pine likes people to do, even now, after all the things that have happened, for he doesn't like to be with others too much. What he really likes is to be by himself.

He was by himself on the day he found his great red hat. He was sitting at the top of his tree, the big white pine in the curve of Sorry road just where the wood turns off toward the bay, and he was quite invisible, looking like one of those large, dark growths that trees sometimes have. Hugh Pine felt good. He had eaten well, and he was just sitting, leaning against a branch with his short thick tail, holding on to the pine's trunk with his strong front paws.

2

But then Hugh happened to look down and saw the great red hat. He looked at it for a while, and while he looked, he thought, *I want that hat.* He began to climb down slowly, for he doesn't like doing anything quickly. *Just what I need,* he thought as he sat at the side of the road for a while to make sure there weren't any cars coming. *If I put that hat on I'll be safe.* He crossed the road, grabbed the hat, and

humped back. He didn't run, for, like all the others of his kind, he had never learned to run.

He sat down at the foot of his tree and put on the hat. When he saw that it fitted his small head exactly, he gave a kind of small roar to show his pleasure, and then he got up and the hat fell off.

So there he was. Back where he had been all his life. A porcupine without a hat. An animal thirty inches long (although he looks longer because of his thick, bulging coat), in danger of losing his life any time he gets on the road, because a car may drive over him and leave him stone dead. A stone-dead porcupine with four stubby legs pointing at the sky.

Hugh Pine grunted bad-temperedly. It had seemed such a good idea when he was up in the top of the tree. With the great red hat on his head, the cars would see him, and they wouldn't drive over him. He looked at the hat lying on the fir needles near his feet. *On the head. It has to be on the head.* He got up, grunted again, and kicked the hat. Then he sat down again and thought some more.

After a while, he put the hat in his mouth and carried it to the white pine. Leaning against the tree's trunk, he put the hat back on his head. It didn't fall off. Good. But it would fall off again if he stopped leaning against the trunk.

4

He knew what he had to do now, but he didn't like what he knew. He would have to learn how to walk on his hind feet, and that's an awkward business for a porcupine.

Now there's one very important characteristic all porcupines have, and that's stubbornness. If there's something a porcupine really wants, he'll get it, even if it's a piece of rye bread you've left on your kitchen table. He'll get in through the window and grab it and waddle right out the door, while you stand there hopping up and down screaming at him. You can break the broom on his back and he'll still waddle on, waving his tail at you, and his tail is nothing to be sneezed at. It's thick and strong and full of sharp quills that will stick in the broom handle so that you'll need a pair of pliers to get them out.

No, there's nothing to stop a porcupine when he has made up his mind about something. And Hugh Pine had made up his mind. He wasn't going to be run down by any car. But he still wanted to use the road, for it's nice to walk on the road, much quicker than ambling about in the woods. He didn't want to be on the road all the time, but he wanted to be on the road whenever he felt like it, and he didn't want to feel nervous and jumpy there.

So Hugh began to practice walking upright, right there and then. He fell down and he got up and he fell down and he got up. But he kept trying. He found another tree, not too far from his own, and walked from one tree to the other and back again, over and over and over until he got sleepy. Then he climbed back into his tree, found his favorite branch at the top, and fell asleep. He held the hat in his lap while he slept, and when he woke up he took it down and started practicing again. After a few days he

could do it. Hugh Pine could walk. He walked to the road and started on his way to the bay, keeping to the extreme left so he could see the cars coming. When a car came and the man driving it waved, Hugh raised his right front paw and waved back. He nearly fell over when he did it, but he managed to stay on his feet.

And then he grinned. He *had* done it. He had walked on the road, and a car had come and he hadn't had to jump for his life. The man in the car never thought about it much. He had seen a little old man walking along under an enormous floppy felt hat. That wasn't very strange. People wear all sorts of clothes these days. Funny hats, big overcoats reaching down to the ground: what's so unusual about that? People are free to look as they like, aren't they? But the man in the car *had* wondered who that little fellow in the big red hat might be. What could be his name?

Hugh Pine didn't have a name then. This is how he got his name.

Chapter Two

HUGH PINE HAD always lived in the woods, and though the woods were wild they were often visited by loggers who went out and chopped trees down and rumbled about on their tractors. In between they had coffee in the morning and more coffee for lunch and coffee again later in the afternoon. And with their coffee they ate sandwiches made out of homebaked bread and fresh butter. Sometimes they brought apples or blueberry muffins. Hugh Pine would smell the the food and become hungry and curious. He would shuffle around, getting closer and closer to the people, until he was right next to their feet, hidden under a bush or stuck away behind a wheel of a tractor. He only wanted the food, but it sometimes took a long time before he could grab it, and while he waited for the right moment to come along he just sat and listened.

Gradually he began to understand what the loggers were saying. They never used too many words, so it wasn't difficult; and just for fun, late in the evening as he sat in his tree and looked out on the world, he would repeat the words to himself and make up sentences until he fell asleep. Once he heard the word *porcupine,* and understood that it referred to him, but he didn't like the "porc" part of it.

Pork, he had learned, is something people eat, and he didn't want to be eaten, so he forgot that part of

his name and remembered the rest. First he called himself Kyu Pine, but that changed into Hugh, and this is how that came about.

One evening he was walking along the side of the road on the way back to his tree, when a car stopped. At first he went on walking, but the car began to move again alongside him. The window opened and a man said "Good evening."

Hugh Pine said "Good evening" too. It was the first time he had ever spoken to anybody, except to other porcupines, and he was surprised he could do it. But then, after all, he had often spoken to himself using human words, so why shouldn't he be able to speak to people?

"Excuse me, old-timer," the man in the car said, "but I have lost my way. Do you know where Rotworth is?"

"Sure," Hugh Pine said. "Straight ahead, can't miss it."

"Thank you, old-timer," the man said. "Say, what's your name?"

"Kyu Pine," Hugh Pine said.

But the man didn't hear him properly. "Hugh Pine, huh? Well, thank you very much, Hugh."

And so he got his name, and all the people in Rotworth knew him by that name and shouted "Hallo, Hugh" as they drove past him, for the man in the car had stopped in Rotworth for a while and told the people there how he had met a little old man on the Sorry road who had given him directions.

"White whiskers, long coat, big red hat."

"We know him," the people from Rotworth said. "Sure do, lives in the Sorry woods, what did you say his name was?"

"Hugh Pine. Didn't you know?"

"Sure," the people from Rotworth said. "Hugh Pine, yup, that's the old fellow's name."

Chapter Three

IF HUGH PINE had been the only one of his kind around, maybe nothing more would have happened, although a porcupine passing himself off as a human being and wandering around on the Sorry road is in itself enough of an event to be remarked upon. But he wasn't, not by any means. He was the biggest porcupine around, and he was the cleverest, but there were a few hundred others, 384 at that particular time, to be exact, all living near the bay and in the woods surrounding Rotworth. And they were all in danger of losing their lives because of the cars that didn't stop until it was too late. Every time that happened there was another dead porcupine.

The porcupines became very frightened of the terrible cars racing along the road, and one evening, when the moon was full and the wind still, they all met in the glade close to Sorry where porcupines have been meeting in times of stress ever since the world was still a place of dreams.

Hugh Pine didn't go to the meeting, though he had heard about it. Nothing had been bothering him lately, and he hated crowds. He just sat in his tree and looked at the tops of the aspens and the birches and the tamaracs below him and felt peaceful. The moon was round and tinged with yellow and orange, and the forest was dipped in whites and blues, and he had had a lot to eat that day. Everything was just the way he liked. In fact it was even better, for the loggers had brought out a big pecan pie that afternoon, and Hugh Pine had made away with half of it. The sweet taste was still in his mouth. Hugh Pine was happy, but he wouldn't stay happy long.

Suddenly there was a scratching at the pine's bark, and he heard the funny tinkling sound porcupines make when they rustle their quills.

Hugh Pine stayed very still. Maybe they would go away. But the noise only got worse. They were shouting and banging on the tree.

Hugh Pine snorted. He began to climb down, slowly and ponderously, snorting all the way from the highest branch to where the trunk of the pine leveled with the ground.

"Yes?" he asked and faced the three porcupines who had been hollering and shouting.

"We are the committee," the three porcupines said.

"Very nice," Hugh Pine said. "How very good of you to be the committee, and how very good of you to come and see me. Why don't you go away?"

He began to climb the tree again, but the committee humped around and set up such a din that Hugh Pine grunted hopelessly and slid down again.

"Yes?"

"We had an emergency meeting," the biggest of the three porcupines said, "and we discussed the calamity."

Hugh Pine ripped a piece of bark off the tree and put it in his mouth. He closed his eyes and began to chew.

"You know what the calamity is, don't you?" the porcupine asked.

Hugh Pine swallowed. "No," he said.

"We are dying out, we are getting knocked over and driven over and *smashed*."

"Aha." Hugh Pine tried to sound uninterested, but he did care, and the care showed in his voice.

"You know the Spike twins?" the other porcupine asked. "The two fellows who moved into the glade behind the nine birches across the road?"

"Yes."

"A van got them. BATCH BATCH! They are in the ditch now, and the ravens are eating them."

"No."

"Yes. And do you know the lady who lives where the brook splits, who can whine so beautiful when the moon is up?"

"I have heard her."

"You won't hear her again. She ventured into the road the day before yesterday, and PLOP!"

"No."

"Yes. And do you know the big bashful fellow with the gray streak around his mouth, the one with the very long quills, who lives . . ."

"He is my brother," Hugh Pine said.

"I am sorry."

"Tell me," Hugh Pine said and stopped chewing.

"A big truck," the other porcupine said. "Yesterday. This must be a bad time of the year for us, a particularly bad time. The truck came rushing down the hill and your brother hadn't quite made it to the other side, and VOPSCH!"

"He should have worn a hat," Hugh Pine said sadly. "You should all wear hats, and not just any sort of hats but *red* hats, *big red* hats. And you should walk upright, and you should walk on the left side of the road, so you can see the cars coming, and you must wave. People wave back. People are all right."

"Yes," the smallest porcupine said, "but their cars aren't. The cars go so fast that *whoosh,* there they are. And you are underneath them. And you are dead."

"I am not dead," Hugh Pine said. "I wear a red hat and I . . ."

"We know, we know," all the porcupines said at the same time, "but we can't do that, you see. We tried but we can't. We don't have hats, and even if we had hats, we . . ."

"You are stupid," Hugh Pine said.

"We are," the three porcupines said, "but you aren't, and you must help us. We decided tonight. We are the committee, and we have come to tell you that you must help us."

"How?" asked Hugh Pine.

"We don't know. *You* know."

He sat down, and the three porcupines sat down opposite him. They stared at each other, the committee waiting while Hugh Pine thought. The littlest porcupine had very shiny whiskers and dark round soft small ears. Hugh Pine looked at her, but he didn't see her. He was thinking.

Hours passed. The moon went away and the sky lit up with the first rays of the great sun.

"Right," Hugh Pine said. "Go away now. Perhaps I know something. I'll go and talk to the people. Not to all of them, to one of them."

"I'll talk to Mr. McTosh. The loggers often mention him. He is very important because he owns the post office. I don't know what the post office is, but I'll find out. I know some words the people use. And I know Mr. McTosh, we have waved at each other. He looks a little like us. He isn't as big as the other people, and he hasn't got a neck, and he has white whiskers, and he even wears a hat. His hat is red, like mine. I'll go and talk to him and see what I can do. Are you quite sure you can't learn to walk upright and walk on the left of . . . ?"

"Quite sure," the three porcupines said and got up.

Hugh Pine looked at the big white pine. He badly

wanted to climb it and sit in its top and fall asleep. The three porcupines had left; he heard them moving away from him in the undergrowth.

Hugh Pine sighed and walked to the road. He put on his hat, got on his hind legs, and began to walk to Rotworth. It was a long way, and he walked all morning, waving at the people in the cars who greeted him.

When he got to Rotworth he looked into all the buildings until he found Mr. McTosh. He sighed once more and went in.

Chapter Four

"MORNING," MR. McTOSH said. "You must be Hugh Pine. I have heard about you. How are you?"

"I am fine."

"Good. It's a lovely day. Do you want some stamps?"

"No. I want a word."

Mr. McTosh leaned over his counter and looked at the little old man facing him. He looked very sharply and took a deep breath. Then he went into the back of the post office, found his glasses, and, putting them on, came back again.

"Yes," he said slowly, "I thought so. So that's why we never see you in town. You don't need anything from the stores, and you don't need anything from me. You are a porcupine, and you live in the woods. You have everything out there you could wish for."

"I need something," Hugh Pine said, "and I came to tell you about it. I need a word with you."

"A word." Mr. McTosh took off his cap and scratched his bald head. Then he tugged at his whiskers and put his cap on again. "A word, hey? I don't have many words, all I have is a lot of stamps."

"I don't know what stamps are," Hugh Pine said.

"You wouldn't want to know. There are so many of them, and they are all different, and they cost money. You don't want to know what money is either. What's this word you want, Hugh?"

Hugh Pine looked around. He was feeling a little desperate now, though he was usually a calm animal.

He just went his own way, plodding along quietly through the woods, ripping a bit of bark here and there and looking for the places where he had ripped the bark before, because there might be a few drops of good sugary syrup to lick. Right now he wanted to lick something. He saw Mr. McTosh's ax standing against the counter, so he ambled up to it and licked the beautifully curved handle. It tasted salty, and if there's one thing porcupines like more than sugar, it's salt.

Mr. McTosh waited. He sipped some coffee from the mug that had been standing next to the stamp book and swallowed. Then he narrowed his eyes behind his halfglasses and watched as Hugh Pine, now through with licking, bared his big orange teeth.

"Ho!" Mr. McTosh shouted. "You aren't going to *eat* that handle, are you?"

Now that was just what Hugh Pine had had in mind.

"Have something else," Mr. McTosh said. "What would you like?"

Hugh Pine looked around him. There were no trees in the post office, and no shrubs. And no mushrooms. But he did want to eat something; he had spent a lot of energy that morning.

Mr. McTosh looked about too. There was an old

pair of boots in a corner. "Do you like boots?" he asked. "I usually go home for lunch, so there's nothing here but coffee and those boots. How about a boot and some coffee?"

"Please," Hugh Pine said; and after Mr. McTosh had poured half his coffee into one of the boots, Hugh Pine ate it, crunching and tearing, smacking and slobbering.

"There," Mr. McTosh said when Hugh Pine was done. "Now what's the word you want with me?"

Hugh Pine took a very deep breath. This was going to be the most difficult part of his expedition. If only Mr. McTosh could understand the grunts and garbles and little snorts porcupines use to express themselves. But of course he couldn't. So Hugh Pine took off his hat and put it on a chair and walked to the middle of the empty post office and began. He used the few words he had learned from listening to the loggers, and he made frantic gestures with his paws and stood on one leg. He got so excited he dropped to the floor and rolled over a few times, but he never stopped talking until he had said it all.

"Yes," said Mr. McTosh a little later, when Hugh Pine was done. "Quite."

Hugh Pine looked at Mr. McTosh.

"Hm," Mr. McTosh said.

"They are stupid," said Hugh Pine. "They can't walk upright, and they won't stick to the left side of the road because they can't remember what left is. And they don't have hats, and if they did have hats, the hats would fall off their heads. That's their trouble."

"Not your trouble," Mr. McTosh said. "You are smart."

"Very," Hugh Pine said and took a piece of the other boot.

Mr. McTosh didn't have any coffee left, but there was still some cream, and he poured that into the boot. "So what now?" he asked.

"Don't know," said Hugh Pine.

"But I thought you said you were very smart?"

Hugh Pine stopped eating. He turned around and faced Mr. McTosh. His nearsighted eyes blinked as he stared at the old man who was leaning on the counter and whose white whiskers hung down onto his folded arms. "I am a very smart *animal*," Hugh Pine said, "but you are a man. And men are smart in other ways. The loggers say you are smarter than most, and you look a little like me, so . . ."

Hugh Pine sat down, using his thick bristly tail as a brace. His long dark hairs waved about in the draft that came through the crack of the door. He looked like he had never combed or washed in his life, but he also looked quiet and determined. Mr. McTosh grinned, because it had suddenly occurred to him that looking at Hugh Pine was a little like looking in a mirror.

"Yes," Mr. McTosh said. "We look alike. And we are both officials. They come to us when they are in trouble, and we take care of it. Not because we like to muddle around and do things, but because they expect us to do something. I have an idea."

"An idea?" Hugh Pine asked.

"Like a word, the word you wanted to have with me. Go and find out which part of the woods the porcupines like best, and then come and tell me."

A draft suddenly blew through the crack of the door, and the long hairs on Hugh Pine's back waved sharply and all his spines came up, making him look much bigger.

"And then," Mr. McTosh said, "I'll come out with some people and we will build a fence, a good high fence, so that the cars can't get through it."

"Good," Hugh Pine said. "Thank you for the boots and the coffee and the cream." He waddled to the door, and Mr. McTosh came and held it open for him.

"Must be more than three feet high; four feet, maybe," Mr. McTosh said to himself as he watched

Hugh Pine walking down the street, very straight under his big floppy hat. *I am five feet,* he thought, locking the post-office door. He got into his car to drive home for lunch, and on the way home he saw a porcupine lying at the side of the road. He was about to drive on, but he stopped, turned back, and got out.

Mr. McTosh stood at the side of the road and studied the dead porcupine. "Amazing," he said softly. "It looks like me. Same sort of face, whiskers and all. I never knew I looked like a porcupine. And I could understand Hugh Pine's talk, too. Amazing, absolutely amazing."

Chapter Five

HUGH PINE DIDN'T walk very far. As soon as he got to the woods he whipped off his hat, dropped down on all fours, and shuffled into an opening in a big patch of raspberries. He found a hollow apple tree and rolled up his hat and hid it carefully, and then he moved his short bristly bulk into the tough plants laden with tasty red fruit and began to eat. The juice ran down his chest, and he had to rub his quills against the bark of an oak, to clean them. The bark of the oak looked fine, so he ate some of that as well.

When he was quite full, he found a fifty-foot pine and climbed it. It wasn't as comfortable as his own white pine, but it was good enough. He was alone. Nobody was bothering him, and he didn't have to think of any difficult words.

Because the pine was new to him, it took him quite a while to find the right spot. He had to have a fairly thick branch to rest his tail on and a fairly flat piece of trunk to rest his back against, and there couldn't be too many small branches loaded with needles, for then he wouldn't have a view. He squirmed about until all the conditions were met. Then he gurgled with pleasure and wriggled his toes.

Below him the wind breathed through the forest of birches and pines and spruces and alders and made it sway like a vast green sea. A raven glided past and croaked deeply and softly, some seagulls planed high above him, and the striped sparrows sang their four-toned song. A squirrel whirred. Hugh Pine listened. The sounds became thinner and thinner, and then, suddenly, his body quivered and he was asleep.

Hugh slept all afternoon and all night and woke up only when the first sunlight stroked his face and made his whiskers tremble.

Then he climbed down, found his hat, and moved on to his usual grounds, where he began to feed around the great white pine. There the committee found him later in the day and heard the news that they had to select the woods they liked most of all.

"But not around here," Hugh Pine said. "Not around this great white pine. I like a bit of peace and quiet, and I don't want all of you trampling about and arguing and shoving. This is my land, and this

is where I want to be, and I want to be here on my own, thank you very much!"

The committee didn't like that remark, and they were going to say something about it, but Hugh Pine looked fierce. He raised his tufted eyebrows and turned around, shaking his tail, which looked like a sizable warclub; he then turned back again, scowled, and bared his orange teeth.

"Yes," the committee said. "Quite. We see what you mean."

"And I want some thanks," Hugh Pine said. "I had to walk forever to meet the chief of the people, the terrible Mr. McTosh, and I took a big risk, for he might have pointed something at me, and he might have banged, like the people do sometimes when they are after deer or birds or jackrabbits."

"Yes," the committee said. "But he didn't."

"He didn't," Hugh Pine said, "because I talked to him and because I helped him get rid of his old boots. So run along, and come back and tell me where these wonderful woods are where you want to live, and thank me before you go."

"Thank you," the committee said and scuffled off, grunting and grumbling and nibbling and stopping off to eat some raspberries on the way.

Chapter Six

HUGH PINE HAD some peace and quiet for a while, for the committee ran into a bit of trouble. It turned out that every porcupine liked a different part of the woods, and there were a lot of meetings and a lot of stumping about. They snorted and snarled, and it even came to fights — fistfights of course, for porcupines use their tails only when nothing else works and when they are cornered and in danger of losing their lives. The spines on their tails are loose and come off when they hit something. They are like little arrows, full of sharp nasty barbs, which can travel right through somebody's body and cause all sorts of damage.

So when porcupines get cross with each other, they sit on their dangerous tails, using them like the legs of a chair, and hit each other with their fists. That doesn't hurt so much, and it still looks impressive.

And while everybody was snorting and shouting and boxing, the committee ran around and broke up the fights and tried to get them all to sit in a circle and speak one at a time. But every time they almost had the circle arranged, some of the porcupines would wander away and go and eat something.

Finally, when the committee threatened to give up, the porcupines remembered that the matter was serious and finally, finally, they all agreed; they sent the fastest porcupine (who was quite slow, really, but much faster than the others) to climb a big tree on a high hill. He shouted down to them, describing what he saw, and they made a sort of map by scratching lines in the sand. The part inside the lines was the woods where they wanted to live.

The committee went to look for Hugh Pine again, and they told him what they had done. He didn't quite understand what they meant, but he came back with the committee and studied the scratched lines and listened to their explanations of what the lines meant.

"Well?" the committee asked.

"You're not so dumb as you say you are," Hugh Pine said. "If you can do this, why can't you learn to walk upright and wear red hats and stick to the left side of the road?"

"We can't," said the committee.

Hugh Pine sat and thought. The committee didn't want to disturb him. He didn't look too happy, but because he never looked too happy the committee had no idea what he was thinking. They thought he was just sitting. But he wasn't.

The fact is that Hugh Pine really felt sad. Here was the committee, all eager and pleased about their map; but soon there would be fences where they had scratched their lines, and all the porcupines would be behind the fences. Locked in. Hugh Pine was a porcupine, too, and he had always been free to wander as he pleased. But then he thought about the Spike twins and his brother Graystreak and all the others that weren't around anymore. No, there was nothing else to do. There would be a fence. He sighed and put on his floppy hat and set out bravely on the long road to Rotworth.

"Hello," Mr. McTosh said when Hugh Pine walked through the post-office door. "Did you find out in which part of the woods your friends want to live?"

"I can scratch it for you," Hugh Pine said.

Mr. McTosh went out with him to the yard behind the post office and watched as Hugh Pine scratched around in a patch of clean sand, explaining that this scratch was a tree, and that scratch was a hill, and all the little scratches were Pobby's Pond, and the line over there was the Burbling Brook, and the other little scratches were the bay.

"Yes," Mr. McTosh said, "I see. I know the brook, that's where we catch suckers in the spring. And there's the beach where we dig for clams, and that big part over there is the pine forest where we hunt deer in the autumn."

"Exactly," Hugh Pine said. He was very glad that Mr. McTosh could understand.

"Hugh Pine," Mr. McTosh said solemnly, "you *are* a smart animal, and I am pleased you came to see me, but this map shows a couple hundred square miles. Your woods are enormous, e-nor-mous."

"Aren't they?" Hugh said. He was still very glad. Mr. McTosh seemed to be understanding him fine. He felt so glad that he got up and began to caper about. Usually porcupines only caper about later in the year, in midsummer, when they feel the need for company and are ready to start their families. But Hugh Pine was an exceptional porcupine, and he liked to break rules.

Mr. McTosh watched and smiled. Hugh Pine's long hairs that hid his quills fluttered and wagged and shook, and the shorter stiff hairs of his whiskers bristled and curled, and the hairs of his thin mustache stood up, and his little dark round ears moved every time he stamped his feet.

Mr. McTosh laughed and Hugh Pine stopped his dance. His teeth showed in a large silly grin.

"Well," he said. "Now maybe you can have the fence built."

"No," Mr. McTosh said.

"No?" Hugh Pine asked.

"No," Mr. McTosh repeated. "That fence would be a hundred miles long. I couldn't ask the people to build such a long fence. They wouldn't do it."

Hugh Pine's merriment was gone. His front paws hung down. He closed his eyes. He felt terrible. He would have to go far, far, far away, so far that none of the porcupines could find him again. He wasn't so smart after all. He sighed sadly.

Hugh Pine with the red floppy hat, the great marvel who could walk upright, had made a promise. And nothing would happen. Everything would go on as before. The porcupines would be crossing the roads and the cars would come, and *wham!*

It would be better if he went away and got lost somewhere, somewhere in a dark forest where he would be the only porcupine around, so that nobody could remind him that he had broken his promise. He might as well go right now and find that gloomy place where the trees would be dead, covered with lichen and old man's beard growing on their rotten, barkless wood.

He moaned and began to stiffen his muscles so he could get up, but Mr. McTosh wasn't done yet. He sat down opposite Hugh Pine and reached out and patted the top of his bushy head, making sure he didn't brush the hairs the wrong way, for he didn't want to expose the quills underneath and get them into his hand.

"Never mind, Hugh," he said. "I would have a fence built, and I will have a fence built. A short fence. A few hundred yards, maybe half a mile. Maybe, if all goes well, a mile. But no more. And look here at this map. Here, you see. Over there goes the road. We'll build the fence along this stretch here, and your buddies can have the land on the other side, as far as the bay here and the pond there. That'll give them some space to run around in, and they'll be safe."

Hugh Pine nodded. "I see, I see," he said slowly.

"Good," said Mr. McTosh happily. "Maybe it doesn't look like much land, but porcupines aren't all that big, and there are plenty of trees in there, and a lot of bushes, and a nice patch of raspberries, and a lot of dead wood on the ground that'll be covered with juicy mushrooms. They'll have everything they want, I am sure."

"Good," Hugh Pine said.

"And we'll start tomorrow," Mr. McTosh said. "We'll bring saws and axes, and we'll cut up some cedars and make posts. It'll be a lovely fence. Just tell your friends to get in there and not to move about too much for a few days, and then, when we go away, the land will be all theirs."

"They won't be able to climb the fence, will they?" Hugh Pine asked, for he knew what would happen if the fence wasn't high. The porcupines would forget all about what it was for and would climb over it into the road.

"No," Mr. McTosh said. "It'll be high, twice as high as I am."

"That's very high," Hugh Pine agreed.

"And it'll be made of metal wire. Chicken wire, we call it. They can climb some of it, maybe, but they'll never get to the top; and just to make sure, I'll put some special wire on the top, barbed wire. They won't want to touch that, because it'll hurt their paws."

Hugh Pine looked at his own paws and turned them over. He wanted to say something, but he blew through his whiskers instead. His quills squeaked as he shivered.

Mr. McTosh was waiting.

"Good," Hugh Pine said. "Thank you very much,

Mr. McTosh." He had some trouble with the "Tosh," but he got it out properly in the end.

Mr. McTosh opened the door of the yard and waved goodbye as Hugh Pine made his way down the road. He stopped a few times to wave back, but not too often, for it wasn't so easy to stand upright, hold on to his hat, and wave all at the same time; and he didn't want to fall on his face, especially not after such a successful meeting.

Chapter Seven

Hugh Pine found the committee when he got back to the woods. He had to run around and look everywhere, and he was quite hot and bothered when he finally found it.

"*There* you are," he said gruffly. "What sort of a committee are you? A committee should be in the right place, and the right place is the first place I look, and you weren't there."

"We are here," the three porcupines said.

"Right," Hugh Pine said, glaring at them from under his big eyebrows. "And here you'll stay until I am finished with you. Listen carefully."

He found a piece of clear ground and a stick, and he drew the map for them, the one drawn by Mr. McTosh, which showed only a little section of the woods the committee had originally included. The porcupines followed the lines with their paws, and they began to snort and grumble so quickly that it almost sounded as if they were yapping.

"But it's so small," they whined. "We'll be all *over* each other. Look! The bay is here, and the pond is there, and we'll only have this little patch next to the road and back to the water."

Hugh Pine got so cross that he turned round and rattled his spiky tail. He tried to grunt something, but he choked on the grunt and coughed until he was red in the face and had to stamp his feet to get some air.

"*That's* what you'll get and *that's* where you'll be happy," he shouted when he had air again. "That piece of land you chose is so enormous that you would

get lost in it. You don't want to get lost, do you?"

"But we've never gotten lost," the committee said. Or rather, that's what the committee whispered. They were frightened of the huge porcupine who stood opposite them, waving his paws and showing his orange teeth, all aquiver with every spike and hair on his body bristling and waving about.

"Be grateful!" Hugh Pine roared. "You bothered me and wouldn't let me sit in my own tree. You moaned and complained and cried. And now, when I try to help you, you give me a lot of silly grunts and garbles. Go away and find all the others. Tell them to go to this piece of land and stay close to the water while the people build the fence around them. They won't take long, Mr. McTosh says."

"But . . ." the three little porcupines began.

"No buts!" Hugh Pine shouted. "Off! Off! Off! Away with you!"

They went away, disappearing into the touch-me-not bushes. The pretty little orange flowers bobbed as they found their way through. Hugh Pine sighed and sat down. But he wasn't done yet. The touch-me-nots moved again, and the smallest porcupine of the committee showed her pointed snout.

"Yes?" Hugh Pine asked.

"Will you be living on that land too?"

"No," Hugh Pine said. "I'll stay here." He pointed to the great white pine. "That's my tree, and it isn't on the map."

"Oh," the little porcupine said. Her snout was still pushed out of the touch-me-not bush.

"Well?" Hugh Pine asked.

"Oh," the little porcupine said again.

"Well, what do you want me to do?" asked Hugh Pine. He sounded sad and tired. "I have my hat, and I can walk upright, and I can stick to the left side of the road."

"And the people in the cars wave at you," the little porcupine said. "I know." Her voice was tiny and melodious and lonely. Hugh Pine tried to think of a good reply. Something kind. Something helpful. But he couldn't think of anything. Slowly the snout of the little porcupine disappeared, and he could hear her rustle away. Suddenly, for the first time ever, Hugh Pine felt just a little alone.

"Bah," he said and began to climb his tree. He found his spot and looked away over the forest to where the green of the trees faded into the blue of the bay. He grunted and began to forget.

Better up here, he thought. *A lot of bother down there,* he thought a little later. And then the thoughts drifted away, and all that was left was a large dark bristly ball high up in the pine, snoring gently.

Chapter Eight

THE PEOPLE CAME and built the fence, and the porcupines watched them from many hideouts and secret places. Their beady eyes gleamed with wonder as the men cut cedars with whining, groaning chain saws and dug deep holes with mechanical spades linked to noisy tractors. They watched as the men rolled off huge rolls of chicken wire and hammered the wire to the cedar posts. Mr. McTosh seemed to be everywhere at the same time, and the porcupines felt very good when they saw him, for he did look remarkably like them, just as Hugh Pine had said.

Hugh Pine was watching too, but from a great distance, sitting in the top of his white pine, swaying in the soft summer wind.

The people were very good. They left part of their lunch and dinner in easily reached places. Mr. McTosh even went far into the woods to hang some big pieces of salt from low branches and then left, so the porcupines could lick the salt without feeling that somebody was watching them. He didn't have his lunch with the other people but walked down the road and waited for Hugh Pine to climb down from his tree. They ate together, leaning against the pine's trunk.

The first day they ate Boston cream pie, the second day they ate strawberry pie, and the third day they ate pecan pie with cream on top. On the fourth and last day, Mr. McTosh brought a choice. He had lemon meringue pie, but he also had a big tin full of salty crackers. Hugh Pine had to think for a long time before he finally decided to eat most of both, for Mr. McTosh said he wasn't so hungry.

When the work was finished, the fence stretched on and on for nearly a mile, starting at the Burbling Brook, extending from there to the edge of Pobby's Pond, and going from there to the tip of the bay. It was rather a forbidding-looking fence, very high and black, and hard to see through because of the fine, strong mesh. But it was everything it was supposed to be, and it would keep the porcupines from wandering into the road.

Before the people went away, while they were standing around talking to each other next to their

loaded trucks, Mr. McTosh and Hugh Pine walked all
along the fence. Mr. McTosh stopped every once in
a while and kicked the fence, and Hugh Pine pushed
it, but it didn't move.

"Well?" Mr. McTosh asked when they had come back to the trucks.

"A very good fence," Hugh Pine said. "A really excellent fence, Mr. McTosh. Thank you very much." He put out his paw and Mr. McTosh put out his hand, and they touched each other carefully. Hugh Pine pushed back his big floppy hat so he could look out from underneath the rim, and Mr. McTosh pulled down his little red cap so he didn't have the sun in his eyes.

"Good luck, Hugh," Mr. McTosh said. "I'll stop by when I am on my way to do some fishing, or maybe on the way back, and I'll knock on your tree and you can come down and have some pie or some crackers with me."

He got into his car, and the people got into their trucks, and they all drove away. They waved as their cars pulled off, and Hugh Pine, standing by himself in the road, waved back.

Chapter Nine

MONTHS PASSED. SUMMER changed into autumn, and the leaves changed color and showed all their beautiful and different shades before they fell off. Then winter came, with a lot of snow and a big gale that shook the trees and ripped at their branches. It flattened the dried-out weeds and roared through the shrubs and the bushes. The porcupines didn't mind. They just held on and waited for the gale to go away. They had plenty to eat and they rambled about, chewing some bark here, digging out fallen leaves there, or pulling out roots and chomping on mushrooms. After the gale they played in the snow, and, later, when there was more snow, they found nice warm places in hollow trees and under rocks, where they could snooze a bit. They weren't troubled by

cars at all. They could hear them zooming past the
fence, but they didn't worry. They knew that the
heavy steel bumpers couldn't possibly hit them, for
the cars could never go through the fence.

But as winter continued, there no longer seemed to
be all that many trees in the reserve. Every time a
porcupine found a tree, he'd discover that somebody
else had been there before him or was actually there,

eating away at the few shreds of bark left. The big rhododendron bushes seemed to have changed into naked skeletons made of thin wirelike branches, and nobody knew what had happened to the mushrooms. Some of the porcupettes, the ones who had been born only a few months before, had to ask their mothers what mushrooms were.

"Things that grow on the trees and between the roots of the trees. Nice white things, and yellow things, and brown things. You can eat them."

But the porcupettes shook their small heads. They had never seen such things.

Hugh Pine roamed about in the Wild Woods, as the porcupines now called them. The woods beyond, the woods nobody ever went to, except Hugh Pine. He sometimes passed the fence, and there he saw the others, with their snouts pushing through the chicken wire.

At first he could see only a few of them, one here and one there, but after a while there were porcupines everywhere along the fence. Some of them had climbed it a few feet and were hanging on by their nails, staring at him. Others were leaning against the cedar posts, and others again were standing on top of each other. They wouldn't look at Hugh Pine when he passed. They always seemed to be looking at something else, and as he moved along he could hear them muttering behind him. They didn't mutter pleasantly. Sometimes he would suddenly stop and turn, but the porcupines would either look the other way or straight through him.

Now, Hugh Pine liked to be by himself and go his own way, but he had always been friendly with the other porcupines and always returned their greetings if they greeted him first. He had often stopped to play with the porcupettes, when they happened to cross his path, and he had always taken time to listen to the older porcupines, who sometimes visited him under the white pine. Now he began to avoid the fence.

But one day, when Hugh set out to have a look at the bay, he found that he was getting close to the fence, and although he thought about turning away, he didn't after all. He just plodded straight on.

When he came to the fence, he saw that it was lined with porcupines, all looking away as he passed. He snorted and burbled and stared at them one by one until he found the small porcupine that had been on the committee.

"HAGRUMPH," he said, so loudly that the little porcupine nearly fell over backward.

"YOU DO KNOW WHO I AM, DON'T YOU?" Hugh Pine shouted.

"Yes," the little porcupine said. She began to scramble away, but he hagrumphed again, even louder than before, and she stopped and turned.

"Why are you standing there all the time?" he asked. "Every time I come near the fence I see all of you pushing and hanging around. Why don't you go into the woods and walk around and do things?"

"Nothing to do," the small porcupine said, her eyes gazing at him dully. "And we are a bit hungry, too. We can see the trees on the other side of the road, they are full of good bark. And the rhododendrons still have all their leaves. I think there are mushrooms over there, too. I can't see them from here, but I can smell them."

"Yes," Huge Pine said, "I'll bring you some."

"No. You'd have to bring some for the others, too, and there are hundreds of us here. I wish we could go and get them ourselves."

"Go across the road?" Hugh Pine asked, his voice grumbling angrily. "What do you mean? You'll get killed! There are cars on the road! There is a car now."

A car whooshed past, and Hugh Pine waved at it.

"Yes," the small porcupine said. "I know. How have you been? We don't see you very often now, not since you got us locked up in here!"

"All right," Hugh Pine said. "I found some good spruces on the other side of the Burbling Brook. They are very fresh and green, and the bark is juicy . . ." He stopped himself and shook his head until not only his quills but even his whiskers rattled.

"WHAT DO YOU MEAN? *I* didn't get you locked up in there. *You* got yourself locked up in there. Don't you remember? You were on the committee, weren't you?"

He was going to say a lot more, but the little porcupine sniffled, and her nose trembled, and her eyebrows sagged until they hung over her eyes.

"Hmm," he said.

The other porcupines had gone away by now. Only Hugh Pine and the little porcupine were left, facing each other through the fence. Hugh Pine put out his tail and leaned backward until it stuck into the frozen snow.

"Why don't you come out?" he whispered after a while. "Maybe there is a piece of loose wire somewhere. You can sneak out and find yourself a tree near my white pine. If you are careful and don't rush about too much and remember not to cross the road . . ."

The little porcupine tried to smile. "That would be nice," she whispered back. "But what about the others?"

She pointed. From where they sat they could see at least fifty porcupines ambling about slowly in the distance, or just sitting and staring at the snow. Hugh Pine didn't want to look at them. He looked at the fence instead. The sun caught the shiny metal of the barbs and made it glint.

"Yes," he said. And that's all he said. He got up, turned, and walked away. When he found his tree, he climbed it and sat on his branch and looked at the forest below, which was covered with fresh white snow. He looked further and saw the frozen bay. He could see the little black houses the fishermen had built on the ice, and he knew Mr. McTosh was in one of those little black houses.

Hugh Pine groaned. He began to climb down very slowly. Very *very* slowly. He knew what he had to do. But he didn't want to do it. He wanted to sit in his white pine. It was the right day for sitting in his pine. But he knew that there was no way to avoid doing what he had to do.

He walked toward the bay again and passed the fence, trying not to see the other porcupines. They pretended not to notice him either, but once he had passed they all climbed as high as they could, to see where he was going. They saw him become smaller and smaller, until he was just a little black line with a red dot on top, far away on the glistening ice.

"What is he doing on the ice?" they asked each other. "There's nothing to eat there."

"He is going to save us," the little porcupine said.

"Really?"

"Sure," the little porcupine said.

"He saved us before, and look what happened to us."

"He is going to save us," the little porcupine repeated. "I *know* he is."

Chapter Ten

"HAVE SOME FRIED fish," Mr. McTosh said, when he saw Hugh Pine sitting near the door of the little hut on the ice. It was very hot inside, for Mr. McTosh had built a roaring fire in a potbellied stove and was frying a big flat fish he had caught only a few minutes ago through a hole in the ice.

"Fish," Hugh Pine said. "I have never eaten fish." He knew what fish were, of course, for he had seen them in the Burbling Brook, but he had never thought you could eat them; he thought they were just brown or silver shapes that darted away as you looked at them, or sank down until they became part of the water weeds.

"Here, I'll put some salt on it," Mr. McTosh said, and he poured a whole heap of salt out of his shaker and handed over the fish, which had become white all over.

Hugh Pine chomped away. He didn't like the fish so much, but the salt was good and tasty, and he asked for a little more. Mr. McTosh poured it out on the floor for him and watched his friend eat. When Hugh Pine had licked the last bit of salt off his paws, he looked up.

"Go ahead, Hugh," Mr. McTosh said, "tell me what you have come for."

Hugh Pine told him. It took a while, and he said

"iiih" and "achchchrmp" a lot in between the words, but he got all the words right in the end. "It's not the people," he said, tugging furiously at a fishbone that had got stuck in his mustache. "It's not the people at all. I know they don't want to bump into the animals, and I know they watch where their cars are going. But porcupines are so small, and so low, and so slow . . ."

Mr. McTosh was scraping the fat out of the pan while he listened. "Right," he said when Hugh Pine was finally done. He stretched his short legs and opened the potbellied stove to throw in another log. "Nice and hot in here, don't you think?"

"Very," Hugh Pine said and shifted a little more toward the door, where there was a good cool draft.

"So what are we going to do?" Mr. McTosh asked.

Hugh Pine scratched his nose with both his paws at the same time. "Don't know."

"I don't either," said Mr. McTosh. He looked out the little window of the cabin. It was getting dark. He began to collect his things.

"We'll have to go, Hugh. It's getting dark, and it's dangerous on the ice when it's dark. You can't see where you are going, and you can slip and break a leg. Tell you what, I'll give you a lift home and we can think about what we have to do on the way."

They walked back over the ice and got into Mr. McTosh's car. Hugh Pine had never been in a car before. He climbed onto the front seat next to Mr. McTosh and sat up very straight so he could see through the windshield. The car started and began to move, and then it came to a crossroad and stopped.

"Why are you stopping?" Hugh Pine asked. "There's nothing in the road."

"No, but there's a sign over there. See?"

66

Hugh Pine saw a post with some funny scribbles on it.

"The sign tells all the cars that they should stop for a moment, to make sure nothing is coming from the other road."

The car moved again, but Hugh Pine wasn't looking through the windshield anymore. He was thinking very hard. And when Mr. McTosh stopped the car again, at the white pine, he didn't get out.

"You are home, Hugh," Mr. McTosh said.

"Yes," Hugh Pine answered, but he still didn't get out.

"What's the matter, Hugh? Have you thought of something?"

Hugh Pine turned and looked gravely at his friend. "You stopped just now because a funny sort of post told you to stop, didn't you?"

"I did, Hugh."

"And you called that post a sign, didn't you?"

"Yes."

"Can't we have some of those signs on the Sorry road? Where the porcupines used to cross?"

Mr. McTosh drove his car to the side of the road and switched off the engine and looked at Hugh Pine.

"You *are* a smart porcupine," he said slowly. "I could have thought of that, too, but I never did."

"Yes?" Hugh Pine asked.

"Yes. We could put up some special porcupine signs, or just one, perhaps. In a good place, just between the hills, where all the cars can see it."

"Yes!" Hugh Pine said.

"And you would have to get your buddies together and tell them they should only cross the road there. Can you do that, Hugh?"

"Sure," Hugh Pine said.

Mr. McTosh laughed. "A very good idea, Hugh,

and we'll put a picture on the sign. I'll make a portrait of you, that's what I'll do, and then all the cars will know they have to stop so Hugh Pine's buddies can cross the road safely."

Chapter Eleven

THE NEXT DAY was very busy. Hugh Pine got up early and walked to town. When he got to the post office, Mr. McTosh had just arrived, carrying a sign with black dots and spots and stripes on it.

Hugh Pine looked at the dots and spots and stripes while Mr. McTosh lit the stove and put the stamp book on the counter and poured coffee from his thermos into a mug and a dish. He gave the dish to Hugh Pine, but Hugh didn't see it straightaway. He was still looking at the sign.

"Is that me?" he asked.

"No, Hugh. That's just some writing. It's an old sign I got from my friend who drives the big blue car with all the lights on it. You have seen him on the Sorry road, haven't you?"

"Yes," Hugh Pine said.

"He has a lot of signs that aren't used anymore."

"That's nice," Hugh Pine said, "but those dots and spots and stripes don't look like me."

"I'll take them off. There's your coffee." Mr. Mc-Tosh went back to his car and came back with a pot of white paint and a brush. He put the sign against the counter and told Hugh to hold it, and he put so much paint on the sign that the dots and spots disappeared. Hugh Pine reached up and touched it, then looked at his paw. "It comes off a little," he said.

Mr. McTosh sighed. "It will be wet for a while, and then it dries and won't come off anymore."

Hugh Pine licked his paw. He closed his eyes and smacked his lips.

"Not so nice," he said.

"Then don't eat it," Mr. McTosh said. "Here, eat these. I'll put some coffee in them." He gave Hugh a pair of old slippers he kept under the counter, and while Hugh ate the slippers he put the sign in the back of the post office.

"It'll have to dry for a while, Hugh. Come back tomorrow and we'll put your picture on the sign. I'll bring some black paint."

"Just black?"

"Yes, so cars can see it. Black against white shows up real nice."

"I am brown, too," Hugh Pine said, "and white here and there, see, at the end of my quills, and my teeth are orange, and there is some lighter brown here, see, where I have more hairs, and . . ."

"Yes, but I don't have all those colors. Just a minute." Mr. McTosh looked under his counter. "Here, I have a little pot of orange here. I'll paint your teeth orange. How is that, Hugh?"

"Fine," Hugh Pine said. "I'll be back tomorrow. Thank you for the slippers."

"You'll have to tell your buddies about the sign."

"I will, Mr. McTosh."

"Goodbye, Hugh."

Hugh Pine humped down the road. He was in a hurry for the first time in his life. He wanted to tell the other porcupines about the sign. But when he came to the fence they wouldn't look at him, and when he tried to talk to them they wouldn't listen. Hugh Pine was so happy that he didn't get cross. He found the little porcupine and whispered into her ear. He told her where there was a loose wire, and asked her to come along and bring the other members of the committee.

She quickly found the other members, and they went to the secret opening and pulled and pushed until they had made a little hole they could wriggle through. When all the other porcupines saw that they could get out, they became so excited they forgot they were angry.

"Wait," Hugh Pine said, pushing the wire back. "You can't get out now. You'll be running all over the road, and there isn't a sign yet."

"What's a sign?" they asked.

"You'll know soon. I am going to explain it to the committee, and the committee will explain it to you. When I am sure you all understand, I'll let you out."

73

Hugh Pine led the committee across the road and made them sit down and explained what a sign was. It took a long time, and the first one to understand was the little porcupine.

"I see," she said," funny sorts of posts with scratches on them. I've seen them. Did you say that you would be on the sign?"

"Not me," Hugh Pine said. "A picture of me."

"What's a picture?"

"Ooooh," Hugh Pine said.

He sat on his tail and thought. It had seemed so simple when Mr. McTosh explained it to him; but Mr. McTosh had used human words, and, think as he might, he just couldn't find a way to change human words into porcupine's grunts and snorts.

It was a beautiful clear day, and the sun was shining, and suddenly Hugh Pine saw his own shadow on the snow. He jumped up.

"Look," he said, pointing to his shadow, "*that's* a picture."

"A *shadow*!" the little porcupine said. "But I know what a shadow is. Why didn't you say so in the first place? How are you going to have your shadow on the head of the post? Are you going to stand in front of it? And what if there is no sun? When there is no sun, there are never any shadows."

"Ooooh," Hugh Pine said.

The members of the committee were staring at him. "Please," Hugh Pine said. "The shadow will be there. Mr. McTosh will put it on. He is very clever. The shadow will stay on, believe me. Tomorrow you'll see. Right now, I want to make sure that from now on you will all cross the road in the same place. The cars will stop for you, but only in one place, the place where the sign will be."

He took the committee there and made sure they would remember the spot. It was all very complicated, and he had to stay with them, because there were cars on the road and they could only cross when there were no cars. Hugh Pine got very tired, humping about, and his hat fell off every now and then. The members of the committee kept slipping off into the woods to rip bark off the trees, and eat the leaves of the rhododendron bushes, and dig under the snow, and find dead logs with dried mushrooms on them. But finally they seemed to remember the spot, and he took them back to the fence and opened the wire for them.

"I'll come back tomorrow," he said. "Keep the other porcupines away from the hole. I fastened it, but they can easily open it again. You'll have to stay here and make sure they don't get through."

When he got back to his tree, he was so tired he could hardly climb to the top. He fell asleep immediately, but he was up and clambering down again when morning broke. At the post office again, he noticed that Mr. McTosh had two signs.

"I got another one, Hugh. One for each side of the road; and I painted them both white. They are nice and dry now. Come with me, I'll paint your portrait on the signs."

Hugh Pine followed him into the yard and stood

very still while Mr. McTosh worked. He wanted to see what the picture was like but he had promised not to move. Mr. McTosh worked for a long time, staring at Hugh Pine, then walking back to the sign and touching it with his brush, then walking back again. He walked forward and backward and forward and backward, and when one sign was done he began on the other.

"Ah," Mr. McTosh said, "I almost forgot!" He went inside and came back with a small can. He did a little more work. "There," he said at last.

Hugh Pine came and looked. His shadow was on both signs. On one sign he looked this way, and on the other he looked the other way. But they were both the same, and his teeth were very beautiful on both signs.

Hugh Pine sat on his tail and tried to look at both signs at the same time. There he was, coming from two sides at once. Amazing.

"How do you like the signs, Hugh?" Mr. McTosh asked.

"Beautiful," Hugh Pine said. "Beautiful."

Mr. McTosh put two sticks in his car, each one with a long shiny pointed tooth on the end. "That's for digging the holes for the signs," he said.

Hugh thought that was a good idea, for the signs

didn't have roots and he had been wondering how they would stay upright. He climbed into Mr. McTosh's car, and they rode until they came to the place between the two hills. There Mr. McTosh made two deep thin holes, one on each side of the road, and put the signs in.

When Mr. McTosh had finished, Hugh Pine went to

the fence and told the porcupines it was all right to come out. They pushed and shoved each other until the committee and Hugh Pine hollered and shouted for them to stop. They wanted to make sure all the porcupines crossed at the signs. To make sure, they made them cross the road many times.

"Fine," Hugh Pine said. "I think they know what to do now."

"Good luck, Hugh. See you again," Mr. McTosh said. He got into his car and drove off.

Only Hugh Pine was left in the road. All the porcupines were eating in the Wild Woods. He waited all day, but the porcupines didn't come back. Nobody wanted to cross. They went further and further into the woods, garbling and snorting with joy, for there was much to eat.

A few days later someone from Rotworth came and took the fence down, and some of the porcupines crossed the road to have a look at their old land. But they soon went back into the Wild Woods again. Hugh Pine and the committee watched them cross. The porcupines remembered the signs, and everything went very well. The passing cars stopped and waited for the porcupines to cross. The committee cheered and Hugh Pine grinned. Then he ambled off and disappeared into the woods.

By the time winter came to an end and changed into spring, the porcupines had become so used to the signs that they wouldn't even think of crossing the road anywhere else. The bark didn't grow back on the trees the porcupines had been feeding on inside the fence, and the people from Rotworth cut them down. New bushes and new trees grew, and the woods were green on both sides of the road again.

So when you ride the Sorry road now, you cannot tell what happened there, but you will surely notice the signs with Hugh Pine's colorful portrait on them, and you will understand why all the cars drive so slowly between the two hills, and why they sometimes stop. And if you drive the Sorry road often enough, you will see Hugh Pine too. He still wears his red hat, and he still walks upright, so chances are you won't know he is a porcupine and not a little old man with white whiskers and a long coat.

Funny thing, but Hugh Pine never crosses the road at the signs. He sometimes stops and looks at them, but he crosses anywhere he likes.

And if you don't see him on the road, you should look for the great white pine. You can't miss it. It's near the road, and it is the biggest tree around. I don't think you should stop there, but you can go slowly, and if you look up, you may see him in the top of the

tree. If there is a dark round shape up there, then he's home. But he may also be at the foot of the tree, resting his back against the trunk or sitting somewhere close by, with his flat tail stuck to the ground.

Sometimes he isn't alone. But the one sitting next to him won't be a porcupine. That'll be Mr. McTosh, the postmaster of Rotworth. When they are together, it is hard to tell them apart. You can really tell only by looking at their hats. Hugh Pine's hat is bigger. But sometimes Hugh Pine and Mr. McTosh switch hats, and then even the people from Rotworth don't know who is who.

So if you see two little old men in long coats and red hats, sitting near a big white pine on the Sorry road, just remember that one of them is a human being and the other one is not. The one who is not a human being is Hugh Pine.